# Mother's Choice

*Kinky, Dark Romance, Soft Domination, Interracial,*

*Forbidden Seducing Short Story For Adult*

Lana Kendra

it wasn't bought for your personal use only, go back to your favorite ebook retailer and buy your copy. Thank you for acknowledging this author's efforts.

# Table of Contents

# Content Warning

Due to its sexual content, this book is only for those over the age of legal adulthood. There are some topics with a lot of foul language. All of the characters are at least eighteen years old.

# Introduction

Are you in search of an exciting and thrilling book to read? Look no further than this extensive collection of Erotic Suspense book. I offer a wide range of genres, including Romantic Erotica, Fantasy, and Urban BDSM Fiction, to cater to even the most discerning reader. Whether you enjoy Anthologies, Westerns, or Paranormal Romance, I have something to suit your taste. My collection also includes Poetic Folklore, Interracial, Black & African American Literary Criticism, and Gothic Horror for those who crave a deeper and darker reading experience. If you're interested in Futuristic, LGBTQ+, Short Stories, or Lesbian literature, my diverse range of options will keep you captivated. Additionally, I offer Humorous, Victorian, New Adult, and College Women's Psychological Mysteries for those seeking a lighter but equally engaging read. Furthermore, My Fairy Tale Collections,

Transgender, Contemporary Western, Bisexual, and Poetry genres will transport you to different worlds and explore a variety of themes. For my Teen and Young Adult readers, I have a selection of European Geography, Cultures, eBooks, Loners, Outcasts, Mythology, Folk Tales, and much more. With such a wide array of options to choose from, you'll never run out of thrilling and enchanting stories to immerse yourself in.

It is important to emphasize that this content is exclusively intended for individuals who are 18 years of age or older.

# Mother's Choice

After an impressive basketball game, Shaya ran into the house, her face flushed and bathed in perspiration.

He picked an apple from the fruit bowl and exclaimed, "Hi Ma! I'm home!"

With a smile, his mother Galit asked her son, "How was your game?"

"Amazing, I got 17 points, and we won" Shaya replied, "Hey, isn't that the acceptance letter from Zayis Shemen?"

"Seems like it," Galit replied. "I didn't want to open it because I wanted you to have the chance"

Shaya's older brothers had attended a Yeshiva (Jewish school) called Zayis Shemen. Being one of the greatest schools in the area, it was well-known for selecting the best instructors and providing pupils with the best education possible, including both academic and religious subjects. Like his siblings, Shaya and his parents anticipated that he would be accepted with ease.

Shaya cried out, "What?!" and let go of the paper. "I don't believe this... They didn't accept me, Ma"

The moment Galit took the paper from her son, she read aloud to herself.

Salutations, Mr. and Mrs. Schuster

We have made the tough choice to not accept your son, Shaya Schuster, for the upcoming term at Yeshiva Zayis Shemen after carefully evaluating each candidate for this year's entering Shiur Aleph (freshman) class. Shaya would normally be a perfect fit for the Yeshiva, but we had to make this difficult decision due to space constraints and the disparate skill sets of the applicants.

Recognize that your son possesses all the necessary attributes to be a successful Yeshiva student and that this has been a difficult decision. He would have been well at home here.

Regards,

Yisroel Dinowitz, Rabbi

The Dean of Students, Rosh Yeshiva

Galit felt terrible for her son and was taken aback. She told her kid, "Let me see what happens when Abba (father) comes home." Perhaps there is something we can accomplish."

With watery eyes, Shaya silently nodded and walked up to his room, dejected.

Galit was sitting around the kitchen table later that evening with her husband, attempting to decide what to do next.

Mr. Schuster stated, "I spoke with Rabbi Dinowitz, and he said there is just no room and that the decision is final." There was nobody to talk to as I tried to convince him that Shaya needed the kind of atmosphere that only they could offer."

Galit remarked, "I wonder if I could get him to change his mind. He's going to be so disappointed." Perhaps a mother's plea could convince him."

Her spouse remarked, "I doubt it, but it can't hurt to try."

Galit remarked, "I don't want to call him though; I feel like it's too easy to hang up on a phone." I would like a face-to-face meeting in his office. Would you like to follow me?"

Her spouse replied, "I wish I could, but you know how busy I am at work. Tomorrow, I'll take you there, and let's hope for the best.

She was from Israel, and her natural dark olive complexion and slim figure accentuated the black lace underwear she was putting on; she had bought it for her husband a few years ago as a gift, supposedly for him, but she really enjoyed the way it gave her confidence, a feminine energy that made her feel beautiful and sensual.

The next morning, as she was getting dressed, an idea began to form in her mind: what if, instead of pleading her case like her husband did, she tried something different?

She was happy with herself when she glanced in the mirror because she knew that her physique would be her secret weapon no matter what her argument was. If she could pull it off without coming across as overly desperate, she would wear a simple dress and her coat and stroll out the door in the hopes of influencing the Dean's decision.

Just before she entered, Galit took out her lipstick and reapplied it; it was a little brighter and glossier than her usual color, but for what she was looking to accomplish it was perfect. The Yeshiva was located in a small building on a tree-lined street; she had never been there before and was surprised at how unassuming the building was. The middle-aged woman who answered the door was the receptionist.

The receptionist said, "Hello dear, how may I help you today?""

"Hello, I'm Galit Schuster. Could I have met Rabbi Dinowitz? We had some business to talk about.

The receptionist came back a few moments later and said, "Well, let me go check to see if he's available." "Rabbi Dinowitz will be with you shortly"

Galit took a seat and waited, her hands becoming sweaty and a bead of sweat trickling down her spine.

"Miss. Scheuer?"You're going to see Rabbi Dinowitz now," a voice from behind remarked.

Galit entered once the secretary had unlocked the door.

"Miss. Scheuer?"Good to meet you, Rabbi Dinowitz inquired. I have pleasant memories of your boys; they are truly amazing young men. How may I help you now?"

With a study full with books, Rabbi Dinowitz, who appeared younger than his 38 years of age, sat at a desk.

"Rabbi," I said at the outset, "We received the acceptance letter through mail yesterday. As you are aware, Shaya has been quite eager to enroll in Yeshiva. When my husband and I learned that he had not been admitted, we were distraught. Is there a chance we could reverse that choice?"

"There's just not much I can do," Rabbi Dinowitz moaned, leaning back in his office chair. "I informed your husband over the phone yesterday. We are already at capacity, and the Shiur Aleph class is filled. We've already decided, I'm afraid."

"Are you certain that there is nothing to be done?"Surely there must be some way we can make you change your mind," Galit pleaded, leaning forward.

"You seem committed to getting him in," the rabbi remarked, "but I'm afraid I'm powerless to alter the rules." I truly do understand you both. Shaya appears to be a lovely young man. We would throw out our arms to him in a different year. However, we are simply out of room this year.

"I apologize," murmured Galit, "I really thought we could work things out." She pretended nothing had occurred, but she could tell Rabbi Dinowitz had noticed. "It's funny," she added, flipping her hair around with her finger.

"Mrs. Schuster, what precisely are you saying?" he interrupted. What kind of financial arrangement were you thinking of? Really, it's a space issue."

"No," she answered. "It has nothing to do with space. You actually could create place for him if you so desired. The top button she had earlier undone revealed the beginnings of her upper chest, so if you're going to be honest, it's not really a space thing at all. She shifted in her seat and felt the cool air of the room on her skin, but she still pretended not to notice.

"Oh, I'm sure I don't know what you're implying," Rabbi

Dinowitz replied.

"You don't, Rabbi, of course. It's not your fault, she continued. "Maybe you overlooked him until you realized you had no room because he's not as smart as my older boys? Correct me if I'm wrong. And as soon as the class was complete, you discovered you had forgotten about him, but it was too late to make amends." Galit grinned as she saw that Rabbi Dinowitz was having problems maintaining eye contact.

The rabbi stumbled, "I-I assure you, Mrs. Schuster, that is not the case." The space constraints we face and the regrettable coincidence that your son isn't our top pupil are both present."

"I wasn't insinuating anything, I'm sorry if it came out that way," Galit said, uncrossing her legs to give the Rosh Yeshiva a brief view of her thighs as she pursed her still-glistening lips and carefully evaluated her next words. She licked her lips and looked intently into Rabbi Dinowitz's eyes. "I was just trying to imply that if that were the case, perhaps the fact that all his brothers went here might help you persuade the board of directors to make an exception and add a student."

"I'm sure the board of directors wouldn't be very pleased," Rabbi Dinowitz remarked, perspiring a little.

"Not at all? Do they not want the family to stay connected to the Yeshiva?Galit enquired.

They'd do so. But I believe we should think about what might happen if word spread that we were altering our admissions procedure. Numerous complaints would be made, and the school's reputation would suffer."

"Shifting again, she watched him try not to stare as her skirt rode up. If it were to come out, which it won't, and that's a pretty big if. People don't know who you've said yes or no to yet, and this wouldn't be a change in policies so much as it would be an acknowledgment that a mistake was made." You are free to interpret it whatever you see fit.

"Maybe that could work," Rabbi Dinowitz said, moving closer to Galit and his desk.

"So we have a deal, then?" Galit grinned."

"Maybe," Rabbi Dinowitz replied. "Would you be prepared to go above and beyond to make this happen?"

She responded, "Yes, of course," a little taken aback that the discussion had progressed this far.

Rabbi Dinowitz remarked, "That's good. I think you should lock the door now."

What?"I questioned, feigning ignorance of the connotation, Galit.

"Miss. "I have not overlooked your hints, Schuster, that you would like your son to be accepted," Rabbi Dinowitz remarked. And I advise you to shut the door if you want to ensure that he gets a spot in the incoming class. If not, this discussion is ended."

"Okay," responded Galit. "Is that all I have to do?She pretended not to know. "

"That's all it takes," Rabbi Dinowitz stated.

"All right," she replied. "Now pardon me; I have an appointment." She smiled and said, "Have a good day, Rabbi.

Rabbi Dinowitz stood up and shouted, "Wait. Mrs. Schuster, you didn't just walk in here and force me to admit everything I did?"

"What do you mean?"Are you accusing me of anything?" Galit inquired."

"Yes, Schuster, Mrs. You are being accused by me of being a nasty whore who is using her body to gain admission for her son to the university.

Galit hesitated long, as though surprised by the rabbi's

charge. "Rosh Yeshiva, I wouldn't do that!" Galit said."As she shut the door and advanced, she made sure to wiggle her hips to reduce the gap between them.

With her knees nearly touching Rabbi Dinowitz's thighs, Galit positioned herself squarely in front of him. The air was heavy with the aroma of excitement and anxiety, and they both knew exactly what was going to happen.

whispering, "Tell me, Rabbi," Galit put one hand on his shoulder and gently pressed her breasts against his arm. "Is that something you'd like?"If it is, we could maybe add it to our persuasive argument to get Shaya in," she said, stepping between his knees.

Galit took a step closer and pressed her velvety bosom to Rabbi Dinowitz's chest.

He let out an unconscious groan as he felt the overwhelming pull of need. He knew he shouldn't be touching Galit, but he couldn't help but reach up and grab her waist.

She replied by stroking his scalp with her fingers, causing him to purr like a kitten, and he momentarily withdrew to remove his spectacles, setting them down on his desk.

She turned and ground herself into him, grabbing his hands and pressing them hard against her waist.

With a growl, exhausted of holding back, Rabbi Dinowitz's hands caressed her sides and slid beneath her dress. Gasping, she pulled away from him quickly and straightened up, not taking her eyes off him as she slowly undid all the buttons on her dress, until at last her whole chest erupted, making Rabbi Dinowitz's mouth water.

Rabbi Dinowitz's breath caught as she hovered above him, just inches apart, and she slowly removed her bra without breaking eye contact, revealing her perfect breasts with small nipples erect from excitement. They bounced enticingly as she moved towards him, teasing him further.

Her soft moans rang through the office as he nibbled on her sensitive flesh, driving her mad with want. Suddenly, he grabbed hold of her breast and raised it hungrily to his mouth, sucking hard and drawing deeply upon its warmth.

Rabbi Dinowitz was driven insane by Galit's lusty groan as she reveled in the pleasure and misery of his assault, her breath quickening and her own rhythmic movement against him.

"Am I winning you over?She took a time to catch her breath after gasping.

Rabbi Dinowitz remarked, "You're making very salient points. What else were you going to say? I'm still not convinced."

Galit grinned and grabbed at him, saying, "That your pants need to come off".

She worked quickly and deftly to take off his clothes, revealing him below the waist. His big member sprang out excitedly, pulsing with desire. Leaning back in his chair and extending his legs, he extended an invitation for her to give in to her cravings.

Galit crept across the floor in the direction of Rabbi Dinowitz, her hips moving in a mesmerizing way as she got closer. She teased him with promises of bliss as her tongue moved gently over her lips, her eyes burning brightly with passion.

"Well... well..." Galit said, raising her eyebrows and speaking in a flirtatious tone. With a flirtatious flick of her eyelashes, she mocked, "Look at that! Such a beautiful specimen, Rabbi."

She straddled him and eased herself onto his lap with deliberate motions. As her weight descended over him, waves of delicious pleasure shot through his veins, causing him to groan.

Her body embraced him, sculpting itself to fit his own

features flawlessly. Galit urged him to examine and revere her body as she deftly moved his hands over her curves. Rabbi Dinowitz responded by letting his palms glide more easily up her toned thighs, further into the hidden creases of her moist heat.   With a loud groan, Rabbi Dinowitz's manhood flooded into her, his blood pounding through his veins.

As their bodies swayed in a cadence, Galit's grip tightened around him, intensifying the force.

Galit encircled him with her arms, sensing the rippling muscles beneath her fingertips. She took a gentle bite out of his neck, making him gasp for air.

"Let me show you how grateful I would be if you accepted Shaya," she said. Pushing herself off of him, she sank to the ground and grasped his penis.

With well-honed technique, she began caressing him. Rabbi Dinowitz struggled to suppress the need to overreact, feeling dizzy.

She took it deep inside until she felt it strike the back of her throat, around it with her mouth with a practiced ease. She then quickly bobbed up and down while making rhythmic head movements. Rabbi Dinowitz, meantime, was clutching her hair and futilely pushing in sync with her movements. His and hers blended into a primordial symphony.

Rabbi Dinowitz tightened his grip on her hair as he became increasingly engrossed in the sensual spectacle in front of him. He started talking gibberish and pleading for his freedom as Galit exploited her influence over him.

She worked harder, picking up her pace and massaging Rabbi Dinowitz's swollen part. His entire body erupted in electrifying shockwaves with each movement, igniting every nerve ending. The combination of the sensations almost took him over.

Rabbi Dinowitz's face contorted with pain as he balled his fists. Then suddenly he blew up, blasting hot semen hard into Galit's gaping lips. He seized inside Galit's lips, but she milked him dry with her unrelenting rhythm.

Rabbi Dinowitz descended from his euphoria feeling both weary and content. Glancing down at Galit, he noticed her cheeks were wet with sweat and her face flushed with effort. Her eyes gleamed with achievement as she realized she had achieved her goal.

Galit stood up gradually and used the back of her hand to wipe her mouth. Without shame, she met Rabbi Dinowitz's stare and allowed him see the satisfaction that was clearly written on her face.

"Are you convinced now?" she inquired in a cool, demanding manner.

Rabbi Dinowitz paused, seeming to gather himself before speaking again.

He declared, "I think we have a deal." "You can tell Shaya he's accepted" .

"Rabbi Dinowitz, I am so grateful for that," Galit re-buttoned her frock. "Thank you for hearing me out" .

Solemnly, Rosh Yeshiva Yisroel Dinowitz nodded.

"Anything for someone as devoted as yourself" . He answered. "This place isn't simply a building but rather an extension of ourselves, and we must ensure that only the best are chosen for this opportunity."

Galit answered, flashing a contagious smile at Rabbi Dinowitz. "Truly, and I'm glad we came to an agreement that satisfied both of us, although you seemed to get more out of the deal than I did. Perhaps in the future there may be more opportunities for discussion." She collected her belongings and left.

Excited by the news, Galit contacted her husband once more while she was outside. She joyfully said, "Guess what? I got Shaya into the Yeshiva!"

Startled, her spouse showered her with congratulations. "That's fantastic news! How did you manage it?"

Galit gave a knowing smile. "It must've been because I am a mother, and no one can say 'no' to a mother!" . In addition, I believe that having a face-to-face conversation with him instead of merely seeing his name on a paper allowed him to consider his choice carefully.

Her spouse grinned and said, "You're incredible, my darling. We ought to celebrate this evening!"

Galit laughed at the madness that had happened and reveled in her power, yet she agreed entirely, eager to tell Shaya the news.

# Acknowledgments

The Glory of this book's success goes to God Almighty and my beautiful Family, Fans, Readers & well-wishers, Customers, and Friends for their endless support and encouragement.

# About The Author

I've spent nearly a decade penning romantic novels. As a passionate writer of erotica, I craft dark, romantic erotica. Anime Naked Truth Se of Sacred Sexuality: Forbidden Seducing Short Stories of an Erotica Nude Sexy Girl Poster. Alongside Erotic Mystery Fiction, Victorian Erotica Sex, Black & African American Erotica, Euthanasia, Daddy Teaching, Forced Domination, Alpha Monster Cuckold, and BDSM for Adults, there's an Erotic Fiction in Kinky Family. I write dark, sensual romance because I adore the power of darkness and everything that it entails. Romance novels have always been my favorite kind of books, and now I'm writing them. The idea that you will like reading and enjoying my fiction as much as I enjoy pushing the frontiers of sexual pleasure in my writing thrills me more than anything else.

9 781685 223120